W9-DFG-749

THE SNAIL'S SPELL

by Joanne Ryder

Pictures by Lynne Cherry

FREDERICK WARNE
New York London

Frederick Warne & Co., Inc.
New York, New York
Library of Congress Cataloging in Publication Data
Ryder, Joanne.
The snail's spell.
Summary: The reader imagines how it feels
to be a snail.
1. Snails—Legends and stories. [1. Snails—
Fiction] I. Cherry, Lynne. II. Title.
PZ10.3.R954Sn [E] 80-24737
ISBN 0-7232-6197-0
Printed in the U.S.A. by Princeton Polychrome Press
Typography by Kathleen Westray
1 2 3 4 5 86 85 84 83 82

To my cousins,
Brett
Douglas
Eric
Erin
James
Jeffrey
Kelly
Matthew
Meghan
Melanie
Shaun

J.R.

To Bessie Cogan,
my wonderful
grandmother.

L.C.

Imagine
you are soft
and have no bones
inside you.
Imagine
you are grey,
the color of smoke.
SWEET PEPPER
LETTUCE
EGGPLANT
Zucchini

You are shrinking

BEANS
BROCCOLI

smaller
and
smaller
and
smaller.

You are two inches long,
lying on the brown ground
all soft and grey.
Imagine you have no arms
and legs now.
Imagine you
cannot walk or run.

SWEET
EGGPLANT

Instead you glide
and make your own
smooth sticky path
to ride on.
It is easy
to move this way
and it feels
cool and good.

SWEET
PEPPER

SWEET
PEPPER

You have a head
and a mouth
with rows of tiny teeth—
but your teeth are on your tongue!
You eat
by sticking out your tongue
and scraping
tiny bits of lettuce
into your tiny mouth.

BROCCOLI

As you glide slowly
on the damp brown ground,
you touch everything
with two short feelers.

On the top of your head
you have two long feelers.
You can stretch and stretch
these feelers
till they look like
long, long horns.

Your small black eyes
rest at the tips of these feelers.
One eye sees the brightness above.
The other feeler
curls around a lettuce leaf.
Now you can see the darkness there.

But your feeler
touches something in the dark,
something wriggling,
someone alive!
Fast as you can
you pull your feeler back.
You tuck your eye
inside your feeler
and hide it from danger.
Your eye glides
down and down
into your head.

When you feel safe,
your eye glides
up and up
to see your world again.
You are soft and small and slow
gliding up and down
and upside down.

On your back
lies a light, curled shell.
It is part of you
and it grows
as you grow.

Whenever you want to rest,
you have a place to go.
First you tuck your feelers
inside your head.
Then you draw your head
and soft, grey body
inside your shell
and sleep.

BEANS
BROCCOLI
SWEET PEPPER

LETTUCE
EGGPLANT

EDISON TWP. FREE PUBLIC LIBRARY